# ANDY & ELMER'S APPLE DUMPLING ADVENTURE

Written and Illustrated by
**Andrew J. Shoup**

**The Fairborn
Rotary Club**

awakening the magic in you®

A Joint Publication by

The Fairborn Rotary Club          TokoBooks, LLC
*fairbornrotary.com*                *tokobooks.com*

For more information about the *Andy & Elmer's Apple Dumpling Adventure Literacy Project*, please visit the website at
**andyandelmer.com**

Publisher's Cataloging-in-Publication
(Provided by Quality Books, Inc.)

Shoup, Andrew J.
    Andy & Elmer's Apple Dumpling Adventure / written and illustrated by
    Andrew J. Shoup. -- 2nd ed.
    p. cm.
    Andy & Elmer's Apple Dumpling Adventure
    SUMMARY: While starting a business selling homemade apple
dumplings, a young man learns about the virtues put forward by the Rotary
Club: truthfulness, fairness, goodwill, and partnerships that benefit everyone
involved.
    Audience: Grades 1-4.
    ISBN-13: 978-0-9720436-3-2
    ISBN-10: 0-9720436-3-2

    1. Business--Juvenile fiction.  2. Conduct of life--Juvenile fiction.
[1. Business--Fiction.  2. Conduct of life--Fiction.  3. Friendship--Fiction.
4. Honesty--Fiction.  5. Fairness--Fiction.] I. Title.  II. Title: Andy & Elmer's
Apple Dumpling Adventure

PZ7.S558835And 2007              [Fic]
                QBI07-600223

Library of Congress Control Number: 2006908550

Printed by Excel Games Press International

2nd Edition 2/11

10  9  8  7  6  5  4

Special thanks to Dottie Meade for having the vision to present the Four-Way Test in a children's book.

Special thanks to everyone at the Fairborn Rotary Club for their continued efforts in making this project a success.

In memory of my mom, Rosemary W. Shoup — the original apple dumpling baker.

— Andrew J. Shoup

The Fairborn Rotary Club would like to express its sincerest appreciation to
Past District Governor Susan Bantz (2006-07, District 6670). Her continuous support and
occasional advice made it possible to put this book into the hands of children.

It was a beautiful morning as Andy sat beneath his neighbor's apple tree.

"What should I do today?" he thought.

Suddenly, an apple fell from the tree and plunked him on the head.

"Ouch!" he shouted.

Then he picked up the apple and inspected it.

"I know. I'll make apple dumplings."

Andy proceeded to pick several apples – as many as he could carry. Then it was off to the kitchen. He spent the rest of the morning and early afternoon in the kitchen, peeling and coring, rolling and wrapping. It was certainly a big job, but Andy absolutely loved making apple dumplings.

FRESH GROUND
CINNAMON

It was evening when Andy sat down to have an apple dumpling for dinner. There are many ways to eat apple dumplings, but Andy preferred just pouring milk over the top.

"Mmmm. These sure are good, if I say so myself," he stated. "But they sure are filling."

He looked over to the counter at his full day's work.

"There's no way I'm going to be able to eat all of these," he thought. "Hmm. I have an idea! Maybe I could sell them."

# Is it the TRUTH!?

Andy was all excited. He hopped up, ran over to his drawing table, and started sketching a label. "I'll call them 'Andy's Apple Dumplings.'"

Andy was proud of this great idea.

**"*Is it the TRUTH?*"** A voice suddenly came out of nowhere.

Andy was startled.

"Who's there?" He looked around frantically, but there was no one around. Andy sketched a bit more.

# Is it the TRUTH?

**"Is it the TRUTH?"** came the voice again.

Again, Andy looked all around, but there was no one to be seen. Then he stopped and looked at his label.

"Well," he thought. "I suppose it's not entirely the truth. I mean, I made them, but they're not my apples."

You see, they came from his neighbor, Elmer. It was his apple tree.

## Is it FAIR to all concerned?

*"**Is it FAIR to all concerned?**"* came the voice again.

Andy wasn't quite so startled this time.

"It's not fair to Elmer," he thought.

Then, Andy had an inspiration.

KNOCK. KNOCK. KNOCK. There was someone at Elmer's door. Elmer opened the door to find Andy standing there, his arms full of apple dumplings.

Andy and Elmer sat down at his table to enjoy a late night snack.

"I'm sorry, Elmer," Andy began. "I should have asked for your permission before taking your apples."

"Oh, don't worry about it," Elmer replied. "These are awfully delicious. Thank you for sharing them with me."

"Say, Elmer...I have an idea."

Elmer was listening, slurping at the bottom of the bowl.

"How would you like to be my partner? You know, your apples, my baking, and we'll split the profits."

"Sounds terrific," said Elmer. "But only if you let me help and teach me how to bake, too."

"Deal," said Andy. And they shook on it.

They spent another hour or so just talking, getting to know one another better. And later, as Andy was walking home...

"***Is it building GOODWILL and BETTER FRIENDSHIPS?***" The voice was back.

"Why...yes it is," Andy said to himself. "It is, indeed."

The next day, Andy and Elmer got an
early start on their new venture. Elmer
manned the ladder, picking the apples,
while Andy gathered strays. Then, they
were off to the kitchen, where Andy
showed Elmer, step-by-step, how to
make apple dumplings...

..from the peeling and the
coring, to the dough making,

to the sugar and cinnamon mixing,

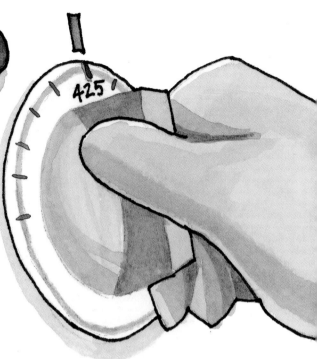

to the rolling and the wrapping,

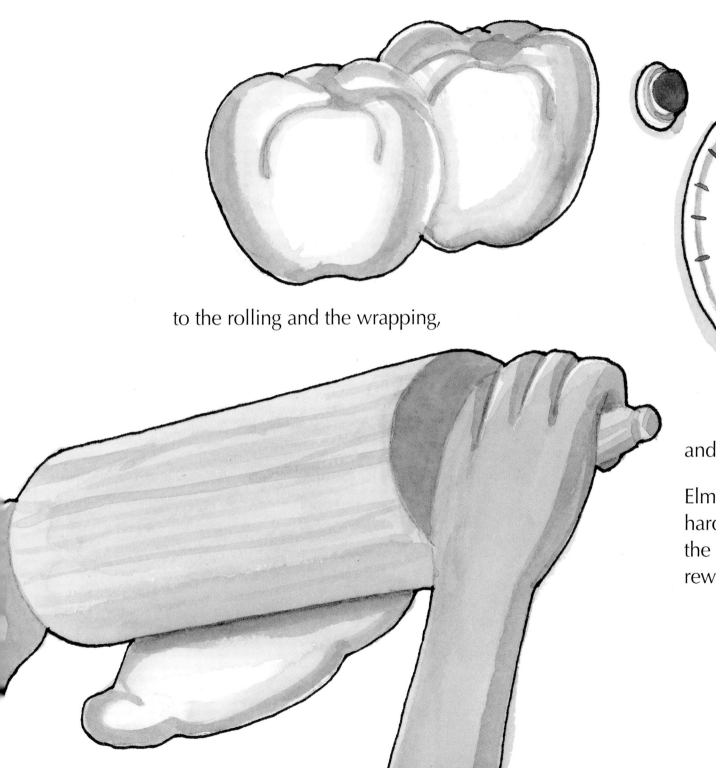

and finally, the baking.

Elmer had no idea it was such hard work. But the aroma of the apples and cinnamon was reward enough for him.

It was about midnight when they put the label on the last package.

"Well, that should do it," said Andy.

"But how are we going to get all of these to the market in the morning?" asked Elmer.

"You've got a point there, Elmer." Andy was puzzled.

BANG! KLANG! CHUGGA! CHUGGA! BANG!

"Hey, I know that sound," said Andy as he and Elmer ran outside.

Sure enough, it was Becky in her old beat-up pickup truck.

"What is that heavenly smell?" Becky asked as she pulled up.

"Oh, it's our apple dumplings," Andy replied. "Elmer and I are going into business together."

"Well, if they taste as good as they smell, you two are gonna be rich," she proclaimed.

"Say, Becky," began Elmer. "Could you help us haul all of these apple dumplings to the market in the morning?"

"That's a great idea," Andy chimed in.

# Is it BENEFICIAL to all concerned?

"Sure, if you wouldn't mind giving me a few," she said.

Suddenly, the voice returned. "**Is it BENEFICIAL to all concerned?**"

Andy noticed that neither Elmer nor Becky seemed to hear the voice.

"We can do better than that," stated Andy. "How about we cut you in on the profits?"

"Yes, yes," agreed Elmer.

"Deal," said Becky. And they all shook.

The next day was incredible. Not only did Andy and Elmer sell all of the apple dumplings, but they had orders for many, many more.

In fact, in the days to come, their venture became so prosperous that Elmer now runs an orchard, Becky oversees a fleet of trucks, and Andy has thirty-two bakers working with him.

And to this day, Andy still isn't quite sure where that mysterious voice came from. Although he now feels that it was simply the voice from inside him, guiding him along his way.

And if you ever visit Andy's kitchen, you'll find posted on the refrigerator, those four little questions to help guide everyone along their way.

Of the things we think, say or do:
1. Is it the **TRUTH**?
2. Is it **FAIR** to all concerned?
3. Will it build **GOODWILL** and **BETTER FRIENDSHIPS**?
4. Will it be **BENEFICIAL** to all concerned?

# ANDY'S APPLE DUMPLINGS

## INGREDIENTS

### FOR DOUGH:

2 cups flour
1 teaspoon salt
3/4 cup Crisco® shortening
5 tablespoons cold water

### FOR DUMPLINGS:

**4 Golden Delicious Apples**
(medium size – approximately 2 3/4" diameter)
1 cup sugar
2 tablespoons cinnamon
3 cups water
1/4 cup margarine

www.**teri**shoots**food**.com

**1** Make some pie dough. If you currently have a favorite recipe, feel free to use that. If not, you can use this one.

Preheat oven to 425° F. Mix flour and salt in bowl. Cut in shortening using pastry blender until all flour is just blended in to form pea-sized chunks. Sprinkle water, one tablespoon at a time. Toss lightly with fork until dough will form a ball. Divide dough into four balls.

**2** Mix the sugar and cinnamon in a bowl. Set aside.

**3** Core and peel the apples.

**Nutritional Information**

*Suggested Child Serving Size: 1/4 Apple Dumpling*

CALORIES 235; TOTAL FAT 12.2g (sat 2.9g, mono 1.4g, poly 0.9g); PROTEIN 1.8g; CHOLESTEROL 0.0mg; CALCIUM 17.5mg; SODIUM 180mg; IRON 0.5mg; TOTAL CARBOHYDRATE 30.4g (dietary fiber 1.8g, sugars 12.6g)

*By substituting Splenda® for sugar, and a light margarine for regular margarine, the Total Calories can be reduced to approximately 179 per serving, the Total Carbohydrates can be reduced to approximately 19.5g per serving, and Sugars can be reduced to approximately .05g per serving.*

**4** Roll out one of the balls of dough. Place an apple in the center of the dough. Spoon some of the sugar/cinnamon mixture into the empty core of the apple. Fill it all the way to the top. Fold the dough up, completely wrapping the apple. Place the apple into a well-greased baking dish. Repeat this for each apple. When you have all of the apple dumplings in the pan, sprinkle some cinnamon onto each one.

**5** Pour water into a pan. Add margarine and the remainder of the sugar/cinnamon mixture. Heat this on the stove, stirring often. Bring it to a boil.

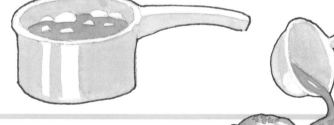

**6** Pour this over each apple dumpling until it comes up halfway from the bottom of the pan. Place them in the oven and bake for about 30 to 45 minutes. Ovens vary, so watch them. Crust should be a golden brown. Enjoy!

# About Rotary International®

Rotary International is a service organization founded by Chicago Businessman Paul Harris in February of 1905. Harris was an attorney who wished to recapture in a professional club the same friendly spirit he had felt in the small towns of his youth. The name "Rotary" derived from the early practice of rotating meetings among members' offices. He gathered six businessmen together to explore ways in which they could better serve the community from which they derived their livelihood and in which they lived. The movement soon adopted a motto; "Service above Self" (1911) and the symbol of a cogged wheel with spokes (1912). Spokes indicate strength and the cogs how working together individuals can create an even greater power. The wheel indicated that individuals and clubs were on a purposeful journey.

Today over 1.2 million Rotarians in 32,000 clubs and 200 countries worldwide carry out Harris' vision. In recent years Rotary has improved the lives of millions through their flagship project, "Polio Plus". Working with the United Nations Health Organization, we have nearly eradicated polio world-wide!

The Rotary Four-Way Test was written by Chicago Rotarian Herbert Taylor in 1932. The company he worked for at the time was in serious financial trouble and Taylor took over as president. He tells the story in his own words:

"To win our way out of our situation, I reasoned we must be morally and ethically strong. I knew that in right there was might. I felt that if we could get our employees to think right they would do right. We needed some sort of ethical yardstick that everybody in the company could memorize and apply to what we thought, said, and did in our relations to others. So one morning I leaned over on my desk, rested my head in my hands. In a few moments, I reached for a white paper card and wrote down that which had come to me – in twenty-four words."

This simple, straightforward test became the guide for sales, production, advertising and every relationship with dealers or customers. Using this yardstick, within five years Club Aluminum was a financial success! The test was adopted by Rotary International in 1943 and since has been translated into more than a hundred languages. It asks four powerful questions:

## Of the things we think, say or do:

**1.** Is it the **TRUTH**?

**2.** Is it **FAIR** to all concerned?

**3.** Will it build **GOODWILL** and **BETTER FRIENDSHIPS**?

**4.** Will it be **BENEFICIAL** to all concerned?

*The Fairborn Rotary Club of Fairborn, Ohio founded May 31, 1931, is publishing this book in honor of their 75th anniversary. They offer it up in the memory of all Rotarians who have lived by the simple, yet powerful words of the Four-Way Test and have sought to serve their local communities and world. It is our hope that parents and children will benefit from the lesson Andy learns: that even in the world of a successful business there are good reasons to care for and about others, and by serving others above self, and following the Four-Way Test, we make a positive difference!*